PRAISE FOR
POISON

"A real page turner that held me in its grip from the very first sentence."

—TOM ROBOTHAM, award-winning writer and adjunct professor of literature at Old Dominion University

"This timely and emotional story is a compelling read, with gripping writing and themes of loss and revenge."

—MIRANDA FAYE DILLON, award-winning author of *The Unshatterables*

"*Poison* is not a book you should read; it is a book you *must* read. Gary Ball unabashedly tackles a harrowing subject that affects us all, either as victim, perpetrator, or wounded witness. The satisfaction that Ball leaves us with is cathartic. I wholeheartedly endorse *Poison*."

—BRANDON CURRENCE, author of *The Bank*, the third book in the *Turtle on a Fence Post* series

"*Poison* dramatizes the all-too-familiar tragedy of a family's destruction as a teenager is entrapped in the downward spiral of drug abuse. Gary Ball brings the reader from a youth's needless death to the consequences of a father's attempts to cope with his grief."

—RAY COLLINS, author of *The General's Briefcase, Motive for Murder, and Setup*

POISON

Poison : A Story Of Loss, Revenge, and Possible Redemption

by Gary Ball

© Copyright 2025 Gary Ball

ISBN 979-8-88824-733-4

All rights reserved. No part of this publication may be reproduced, stored in a retrieval system, or transmitted in any form or by any means—electronic, mechanical, photocopy, recording, or any other—except for brief quotations in printed reviews, without the prior written permission of the author.

This is a work of fiction. All the characters in this book are fictitious, and any resemblance to actual persons, living or dead, is purely coincidental. The names, incidents, dialogue, and opinions expressed are products of the author's imagination and are not to be construed as real.

Cover art and design by Lauren Sheldon

Published by

3705 Shore Drive
Virginia Beach, VA 23455
800-435-4811
www.koehlerbooks.com

POISON

A STORY OF LOSS, REVENGE, AND POSSIBLE REDEMPTION

GARY BALL

VIRGINIA BEACH
CAPE CHARLES

CONTENTS

CHAPTER 1 1

CHAPTER 2 6

CHAPTER 3 10

CHAPTER 4 13

CHAPTER 5 19

CHAPTER 6 26

CHAPTER 7 32

CHAPTER 8 36

CHAPTER 9 40

CHAPTER 10 44

CHAPTER 11 54

CHAPTER 12 58

CHAPTER 13 66

EPILOGUE 69

To all families ravaged by drug addiction.

CHAPTER 1

I NEVER INTENDED TO BECOME A MURDERER. But when the pushers corrupted my boy, then took his life, I had to act.

I had never considered myself a "man of action." Such men were the stuff of movies, adventure novels, and SEAL teams. I was something very different: an English teacher, an assistant professor, an unremarkable member of the faculty at a small southeastern college, where I spent my days amid stacks of books and student essays. So, finding myself staring through crosshairs at an overweight pusher on a littered street corner 120 yards away was a new experience for me. Now I had to decide whether I would squeeze the trigger.

A year ago, my son died in his dorm room just three blocks from where I now stood. Fentanyl overdose. I knew these two words would haunt me forever.

At nineteen he had been in and out of drug rehab three times, including a nine-month residential stint in a high-priced facility in North Carolina that had taken all our retirement savings and left us deep in debt. But once Chris and his doctors had declared victory over his addiction, his mother and I dared to hope again after three years of disillusion, worry, and parental impotence.

Chris—our only child—had been an honor roll student and a speedy, graceful athlete who excelled in all sports, especially basketball and baseball. The high school coaches had counted the days until he could play for their teams, and as a freshman, he quickly won the position of backup point guard behind the school's all-star senior.

Chris's court vision, combined with his speed on the fast break, enabled him to shred defenses, so the coach brought him off the bench to change the tempo of games. In a key game against a crosstown rival, Coach Hughes put Chris in near the end of the first quarter when the team was struggling against a tight zone. Chris quickly hit a three, drove for a layup when the defense overplayed him on the perimeter, then found open teammates for two more baskets when he was double-teamed. Propelled by the shift in momentum, Chris's team won by six and advanced to the state playoffs.

After the game, the coach told Lauren and me that he considered Chris the future of the program.

Though he was just fifteen, Chris was six feet, one-inch tall, 167 pounds, with thick red-blond hair that bounced when he ran. To his mom and me, he was beautiful.

Spring brought baseball season, when Chris's gravity-defying curveball helped his team win the four games he started. Chris helped at the plate too, hitting .297 and leading the team in stolen bases, including a home-plate slide that tipped the balance in a district playoff game.

Chris's success continued through his sophomore year, when he started at the point in basketball, went seven and one as a pitcher, and made all-district in both sports.

Despite his hectic schedule, Chris earned high marks in challenging college-prep courses. He muscled his way to good grades by staying up late when he needed to and studying over breakfast and during breaks in his school day. We congratulated ourselves that we had been blessed with an exceptional child whose future looked limitless.

Then Chris tore his ACL on an awkward slide in a summer rec-league baseball game. The damage was season-ending, painful, and severe enough to threaten his ability to play basketball in the fall.

The orthopedist prescribed Percocet, fifty doses to control the pain until surgery. At the time, we thought pain meds made sense; Chris was hurting, and we trusted the doctor. The opioid epidemic, crisis, whatever the newscasters call it now, was not on our radar.

We had to wait three weeks for the surgery, and in those twenty-one days, Chris took two Percocets every day—and came to rely on them. In addition to the pain, he fought depression. He had experienced no serious setbacks in his young life, and going from a joyful, speedy athlete to a spectator who's every movement was a reminder that he was indefinitely sidelined was a struggle for him.

The doctor assured us that he would fully recover, but complete rehabilitation could take up to nine months. This sounded like an eternity to Chris.

The doctor prescribed more Percocet to help with post-surgery rehab, which began immediately after the operation. Rehab was often painful, and in his drive to recover quickly, Chris relied on the painkillers to help him push through the exercises. We can look back now and see that his determination to return to the sports he loved led him to embrace the drugs, which he viewed as the key to recovering both his health and his hope for the future.

Maybe we had failed as parents to give him the emotional tools to manage a serious but temporary setback. In any case, we didn't recognize how deeply the drug had sunk its claws into Chris's brain.

Because he was young and fit, Chris achieved full flexion and extension in his knee in just six weeks, but the doctor warned him against playing sports for another six months so the new ACL could fully knit. Lateral movement—like that essential to basketball—was taboo, so Chris was facing a lost basketball season. Though he put up a brave front, he was devastated.

With the conclusion of Chris's physical therapy program, the doctor ended his Percocet prescription. When he did, Chris surprised us by complaining that the doctor was holding him back from playing the sport he loved the most, claiming that the painkillers were helping him recover faster. While there may have been some truth in that during the early days of rehab, Chris admitted that he could now move his knee freely without pain, so we agreed with the doctor that drugs were no longer needed.

Chris forcefully disagreed with us, claiming we no longer had his best interests at heart, and began spending more time alone in his room. Lauren and I were mildly concerned but believed he would adjust to the short-term reality of forced recuperation. We felt sure that once the doctor cleared him to play, he would return to the positive, cheerful form that made him so loveable.

Despite the long hours Chris now spent in his room, his

grades began to suffer. This surprised us because Lauren and I had assumed he would use his newfound free time to study. When his first report card came out, though, all his grades were lower than we had ever seen—mostly Cs, with a few Ds.

Digesting our surprise at the falling grades, Lauren and I had a long talk with Chris, reminding him that his forced absence from sports was temporary and wondering aloud if he needed help with depression. Chris claimed he understood his situation and insisted he didn't need any professional help. He assured us that we shouldn't worry and that he would turn his grades around. The talk ended with strong hugs and reassurances of love and understanding.

CHAPTER 2

SO BEGAN OUR DESCENT INTO HELL. The next year brought the unfolding horrors that any addict's family knows too well. Money missing from wallets and purses. Late-night noises and daytime lethargy. Reassuring words that don't lead to promised actions. The awful discovery of hard drug use. The fierce parental determination to do everything necessary to save our child. The rehab, followed by relapses. The sickening swings between hope and despair. The inexorable evaporation of positive expectations.

The soul-wrenching evolution of Chris's addiction culminated when Lauren found him in his bedroom at 12:35 a.m. on a Tuesday, injecting the contents of a syringe into his thigh.

After a failed outpatient rehab effort and two useless weeklong residential stints by the middle of Chris's junior year, we doubled down, finding a clinic in Durham with a strong record of success with young addicts. It was clean, cheerfully decorated, and hideously expensive. I had a solid healthcare plan through the college, but it fell far short of covering the cost. Lauren and I emptied our retirement savings and secured a second mortgage, determined to do anything we could to save our son.

The first signs were encouraging. Once Chris weathered withdrawal, he willingly embraced the program. He earned his GED, racing through the courses taught by caring, competent teachers who came to the clinic daily to work with the dozen or so teens in residence.

He also found love. Her name was Kara, and she was a seventeen-year-old addict introduced to hard drugs by the family's chauffeur, who had disappeared after getting her pregnant. Kara's parents, well-to-do Argentineans involved in the international beef trade, were raising Kara's little boy as their own.

Kara was slim, bright, and vivacious. She reminded Lauren and me of a young Penélope Cruz. She and Chris made a beautiful couple. Lauren and I reveled quietly in watching them tease and flirt as if they were in a regular high school setting. It gave us a glimpse of normal behavior that the drugs had stolen from us, and their love for each other seemed to reinforce their determination to move quickly toward a healthy future together. Chris's positive attitude led the counselors and doctors to assure us that he would soon be ready to return to a life unshadowed by addiction.

Before Chris got out of the clinic, he applied to several colleges. In his application essay, he wrote candidly about his descent into addiction, his recovery, and his determination to use the experience as a motivation to help others as an addiction counselor.

To our surprise and joy, Chris even talked about reigniting the sports career he loved so much. He was determined to join high-level rec leagues in baseball and basketball. He wanted to get back in playing shape and maybe "walk on" to a college team.

A month before the doctors declared that he was fully recovered, Chris was accepted by a small university in a midwestern state about a thousand miles from our home. We all agreed that getting far from Chris's local connections would be wise. He didn't need "friends" who might present temptations that could cause a relapse. Chris had always been vague about his drug sources, and while this vagueness had been a disappointment to Lauren and me, we didn't push the issue, preferring to focus on getting Chris well without the distractions of police involvement or what he might view as a betrayal of friends.

We had been open about Chris's addiction with the parents of his closest friends, his coaches, and his teachers. We believed that knowledge of our situation might help other families avoid or, if necessary, confront similar realities. Sadly, we later learned that Chris was not the only one in our circle who had fallen into addiction. Terry Hardy, an all-district football player and affable, laugh-loving son of close neighbors, had inexplicably dropped out of school in the middle of his senior year and died that summer from an overdose.

For now, though, we were daring to feel that our son had worked his way back to solid ground and had, for the first time in years, the most precious of prospects, a promising future. Kara, too, was succeeding in her therapy and close to finishing her GED. She was planning to apply to the same university Chris was going to attend.

Lauren and I probably looked dazed with happiness when we listened to Chris and Kara share their plans to get degrees, find "great jobs," and start a family. The joy and excitement they radiated began to heal our bruised spirits and filled us with hope.

Chris was home with us for almost a month before he was to start school, and it was the best month we'd had in years. We talked briefly about a beach vacation, but honestly couldn't afford it, so Chris and Lauren focused on shopping for his college clothes, school supplies, and dorm necessities. Chris also pitched in to help me with yard work, car washing, and other mundane activities of late summer. He was cheerful, energetic, and fun—we laughed a lot that month—like his old self. We got into a rhythm of daily life that felt normal and comforting.

Then Chris stopped hearing from Kara. She wouldn't answer or return his numerous and persistent calls. In desperation, Chris finally called the therapy center, where a sympathetic counselor breached the confidentiality guidelines by letting Chris know that Kara had left the center.

Chris and Kara had exchanged addresses, and Chris pleaded with us to let him use the car to go to her home, which was more than 300 miles away. I refused, but because I had Kara's father's business card, I promised to call him. When I did, Mr. Gonzales told me that Kara's mother had taken Kara and her son to Argentina, and they would not be coming back. He would not provide any contact information. While I understood his reasoning, I knew this would be devastating news for Chris.

CHAPTER 3

ALL THIS HAPPENED ABOUT A WEEK BEFORE WE WERE to take Chris to college. We tried to keep his focus on promising possibilities, but he was deeply wounded. As a result, the first day of our drive to his college was mostly quiet, despite Lauren's efforts to divert Chris by playing tour guide along the way. No amount of barbecue or oddball local attractions, both longtime family favorites, could lift his spirits.

Late in the second day of the trip, though, Chris seemed to cheer up. He told us that he realized he would have been away from Kara for a few months anyway while she finished her GED and he adapted to college. They probably would not have seen each other before Christmas, he reasoned. In the meantime, he expected her to reach out to him eventually. After all, his cell phone number hadn't changed, and she knew where he was going to college. Lauren and I were pleased that he had decided to deal with Kara's absence in a sensible, adult way. We felt more optimistic than ever about his recovery.

Our optimism rose even more when we shared Chris's excitement at seeing the beautiful university campus for the first time. The atmosphere at the dorm buzzed with energy as dozens of bright-eyed freshmen and their parents lugged clothes, laptops, snacks, and other essentials into the six-story dorm. Students were already playing Ping-Pong and cavorting in the heated pool as we looked for Chris's fourth-floor room, where we met his new roommate, Carlos. Carlos was from a small Texas town and declared that he was intent on becoming an astrophysicist. He had a ready smile and a happy eagerness, and we all liked him immediately.

Later, Lauren and I treated Chris to a ribeye dinner at a famous steak house and then dropped him off at his dorm with hugs, hopes, and a few tears.

The next morning Lauren and I started a leisurely drive back home. The weight of our worry had lifted, and we found ourselves basking in a sense of accomplishment—we had saved our son, our only child.

On the drive, we began to rediscover each other. We laughed more easily than we had in years, granted ourselves permission to relax, and even began flirting again, just like when Chris was young and the world was a kinder, simpler place.

We were almost home when we got the call from the university police that Chris was gone—dead.

Carlos had come home from morning classes and, puzzled that Chris was not out of bed, tried to wake him. As we later learned, Chris had died from a fentanyl overdose.

Lauren and I borrowed money from her widowed father to fly back to retrieve our son's body. We learned from a local police detective that a neighborhood less than a mile from the university was a notorious haven for drug dealers. The detective surmised that Chris had walked through the area while exploring his new surroundings and had succumbed to temptation.

We arranged to have his body shipped home, where we held his funeral five days later. The crowd of mourners spilled out of the chapel, but the faces were a blur and the condolences just hollow echoes.

In the days following the funeral, Lauren and I were too devastated to do anything but lie around the house, periodically sobbing. After ten days of living on food friends dropped off, I ventured back to work but felt like a robot going through the motions. Lauren took another week before she could leave the house. The world was a different place now, and I felt a darkness I had never known growing inside me. I suddenly realized that belief in a benevolent god was a luxury of the fortunate and the fatuous.

CHAPTER 4

I COULDN'T FORGET A COMMENT THE DETECTIVE MADE: "This happens to too many kids around here." I knew that somebody near Chris's college had sold him the drug that killed him. Pondering this obscene fact, I began to hear the whisper of a new sense of purpose growing inside me, a mission that might give me a reason to continue living.

I decided to try to fight back. People could argue that this notion was irrational, but the idea of doing something, to "take arms against a sea of troubles," just felt right. It gave me a sense of purpose, a release valve for my overwhelming anger, a way to fill the void of impotence. I had failed to protect my son, my only child, but I could act to memorialize his existence.

The famous declaration that "the only thing necessary for the triumph of evil is for good men to do nothing" began echoing in my mind. I didn't and don't claim to be a good man, but I could stand up against the tide of evil. I could bring harm to the scum dealing the drugs that killed my boy.

But I didn't know who they were or how to find them. Nor did I know how to attack them. I was a man of words, not of action. But words wouldn't help.

In my mind's eye, I began to picture myself as a kind of Walter White. He had transformed himself from a mild chemistry teacher into a cold, ruthless criminal. Once I embarked on this line of thought, I experienced a shift in my self-perception. My world had changed, and I was going to change with it. An urge to strike out dominated me—and it felt good.

Like Walter White, I wanted to be effective and efficient but avoid violence directed against me. And, since what I was contemplating would be illegal, I had to avoid the police. Then there was Lauren. I no longer cared much about my career, and friendships felt secondary to the urge to overcome the gnawing sense of failure, but I had to protect Lauren. Whatever happened, I had to make sure no additional harm or grief could touch her.

I decided my next step was to return to the town where Chris had died. I would learn about the neighborhood where he had most likely acquired the fentanyl and dig deeper into who could have killed him. I concocted a story about a conference I needed to attend and traveled during the first week of the Christmas break. I felt bad lying to Lauren, but I wanted to spare her both the worry and knowledge of my actions. If I decided to commit a crime, I didn't want her implicated.

Money was less of a problem now because we had gotten a $50,000 infusion from a life insurance policy we had taken out on Chris years before. We were still deeply in debt but had a little breathing room financially. Nevertheless, I decided to drive rather than fly to my fictional conference. I didn't want Lauren to know where I was going. I managed our finances, but if she wanted to, she could look up my purchases on our shared computer. Knowing that I'm notorious for my hatred of flying, Lauren didn't question my decision to drive. I told her the "conference" was in a city about 200 miles from my actual destination.

Retracing the route we drove to deliver Chris to his college was brutal. Every exit, every landmark, abraded the raw hurt I felt. My son had been alive the last time I drove this way, and now he was not. The world was a different, darker place. But I found that the pain sharpened the edge of my determination. I wanted to strike back at those who took him from me.

After the two-day drive, I checked into a motel near the campus and started cruising the surrounding area. Within fifteen minutes, I found a run-down neighborhood about two blocks south of the campus. It was a Tuesday, a mild afternoon, and there were a few small knots of locals gathered in front of barber shops and tiny markets. Most of the storefront signage was in Spanish, and the leaners and loiterers looked to be young Hispanic men in their twenties.

As I cruised by slowly, some eyed me suspiciously, or so I thought. Maybe they were just curious, wondering why a graying middle-aged man in a car with an out-of-state license was in their neighborhood. They may have been feeling territorial or thought I was a lost tourist or a clueless college parent. In any case, I got spooked and decided I was attracting too much attention.

Trying to find my way out of the neighborhood, I turned right and found myself on a block of stucco duplexes and old two-story frame houses. Some had faded "For Sale" signs in their stamp-sized front yards, and one featured an ancient Ford LTD on cinder blocks. The windows were boarded up on two of the houses. A few cars were parked along either side of the quiet street. The only sign of life was a brindled pit bull chained to a post in a dusty yard about halfway down the block.

Then, near the end of the block, I noticed a stocky man with shoulder-length black hair sitting on a folding chair by the sidewalk under a low, spindly tree.

He looked too young to be a retiree passing the time. He seemed more like a lookout or a guard. Then the thought struck me: he might be a drug dealer. Maybe this was the opportunity I had driven almost a thousand miles for. I pulled to the curb in front of the man and rolled down the car window. The man stiffened slightly and studied me through narrowed eyes.

I have no experience as an actor, and I didn't know what I was going to say, but I blurted, "Good afternoon." The man stared at me. I went on, feeling like a fool, "I was wondering if you could tell me . . . I mean . . . you know, that is to say, where I might be able to buy some drugs . . . for a friend?"

The man burst into laughter, revealing three gold upper front teeth. Wiping tears from his eyes and catching his breath, he finally said, "You're funny, man! What are you, an insurance man with a young girlfriend who likes to get high?"

"No girlfriend. It's for my wife. She's sick."

He was more serious now. "What kind of sick?"

"Cancer. She's in a lot of pain." I wasn't sure where these words came from, but they seemed to have registered with the man.

He studied me for what felt like a long time, then said, "Well, the shit I got will take care of any pain, bruh."

"I want it then."

He nodded. "How much?"

I hadn't anticipated this question, though I realized instantly I should have. I didn't have much cash on me. I said, "Just enough for her to try, see if it helps."

He nodded again, thought for a few long seconds, then clapped his hands on his knees and rose briskly. "I'll be back in a minute."

The man headed toward his house, then paused as I called out to him, "Wait!"

He slowly walked the few steps back to my car. I asked, "How much will it cost?"

"Fifteen. And I don't take checks or credit cards," he said with a snorting laugh that showed his gold teeth.

"Okay."

As he walked toward his duplex, I yanked out my wallet and found a twenty. The man emerged, approached the car, and slid into the passenger seat. He smelled strongly of stale cologne and body odor. I proffered the twenty, and he handed me a small plastic bag with light brown powder in it. He pocketed my twenty, then, from his other pocket, pulled out a wad of cash and peeled off a five—my change.

"Your wife ever do drugs before?"

"A little pot."

"Well, this shit she can snort, smoke, eat, or use with a needle. You want more, I can get all you want. And if you like pills instead, I can get you those too, if I know ahead of time."

"Okay. So . . . what is this stuff?"

"The world's best painkiller—heroin."

I felt stupid saying thanks but said it anyway.

He replied, "No problem, bruh."

He got out, sat in his folding chair, and gave me a wave that seemed oddly friendly. I tucked the baggie into my jacket pocket, feeling like a criminal myself as I drove away. I left the windows down to get his stink out of the car.

I had just met the man who may have supplied the drugs that killed my son. I knew I could never be certain, but he was clearly an agent of the legion of drug dealers that preyed on people like Chris, people who were trapped in addiction. That fact, to me, made him evil.

CHAPTER 5

THAT NIGHT, UNDER THE EFFECT OF A POWERFUL SLEEPING PILL, I had an unforgettable nightmare. In my dream, Lauren, Chris, and I were visiting Lauren's friends from college at their home in Massachusetts. The day was gray and cold, but inside the warm house a Christmas tree and decorations made for a cheery, cozy atmosphere. Lauren and I were much younger, in our twenties. Our friends had gone out to do last-minute shopping, and I was staring into a pine-scented fire glowing in the fireplace, sipping hot cinnamon-flavored apple cider, when Lauren appeared in the doorway to ask if I knew where Chris was. I didn't.

We quickly began a search, calmly at first, then more urgently, worried that Chris, just a three-year-old, was doing something he shouldn't in the unfamiliar house. We couldn't find him. Then Lauren looked out a back window to see his tiny figure standing at the edge of a river.

The river, normally a thirty-yard-wide stream of fast-flowing current, was frozen over, and Chris appeared to be mesmerized by a ragged crow hopping around on the ice. Before Lauren and I could act, Chris started toddling toward the crow. While I rushed to the back door, Lauren struggled to open the window, calling out to Chris when she finally wrestled it up. He didn't respond, venturing farther across the ice and toward the croaking crow.

Just as I exited the house, the ice gave way, and Chris instantly disappeared in the black, fast-flowing current. With the maddening slowness so common in nightmares, my sluggish legs finally carried me out onto the ice, which inexplicably held my weight. When I reached the place Chris had fallen through, I found no hole, only solid ice. The crow, dancing just a few steps away, gave a croak that sounded like a mocking laugh and launched into the air.

Then I awoke, sweaty and shaking. While I never before interpreted a message from any dream, the meaning of this one seemed inescapable. The crow represented the drug dealer who had lured our son to his early death. Perhaps I had found the "crow" and would soon find a way to destroy him.

Over the next two days, I traveled the streets of the neighborhood until I knew every turn, storefront, and alleyway. I bought drugs from two more dealers, who, I discovered, were quite happy to have a new client. One Black dealer cheerfully noted that I was not "the usual customer," but he was happy to "help me out." Both dealers were brazen in their trade and seemed to harbor little fear or even recognize that they were engaged in felonious activity. Both supplied me with baggies of brown powder for less than twenty dollars.

As I slowly rolled through the streets, I studied my surroundings.

If I was serious about killing these death-dealers—and I was—what was my best strategy?

I knew that in movies, gangsters tended to shoot targets from a moving car or even walk up and pour bullets into victims at point-blank range. The drive-by wouldn't work because I had no accomplice to drive my car, and the close-range attack required a boldness I wasn't confident I possessed. In either case, the car I was driving, if spotted by a neighbor or passerby, could lead police or, worse yet, gang members to me.

In war movies, I had seen snipers kill their victims from long range. Distance from the target appealed to me. I decided to learn more about long-range weapons and eventually pay another visit to my new dealers.

Back home, I easily fabricated answers to Lauren's few questions about my "conference." She was still deeply sad, depressed even, and displayed only the slightest interest in my vague responses.

Lauren was a gifted artist, specializing in oils and small sculpture. Our home was a showplace for her art, and she had occasionally sold a few pieces at local galleries. She was also a member of several environmental groups in our area and more socially inclined than I had ever been. Practically all our social agenda was driven by her.

I was an introvert by nature, with few close friends, but I enjoyed her efforts to stay connected and knew that the social situations she placed me in were, by and large, good for me. Otherwise, I could easily fall into self-isolation, which I knew wasn't healthy. My entertainment was based on classic books, old movies, and long-distance running, which I had pursued since making the cross-country teams in both high school and college. Since Chris's drug crisis, though, Lauren's energy for her art had waned, and my running was only sporadic.

In consideration of our loss of Chris, my department head had scheduled only two low-level classes for me to teach, so I had ample time at home to conduct research on the internet. My first efforts focused on analyzing the drugs I had bought. I found test strips online that would change color to identify the presence of more than a hundred drugs. Using these, I found that all the powdery substances I had brought home contained both heroin and fentanyl.

My next research effort went toward learning about long-range rifles. I had never given much thought to guns. They frightened me. Their brute efficiency, noise, and destructive purpose repelled me. But I knew they could kill from a distance, and that quality aroused my interest.

My research focused on hunting rifles, since what I intended was, to my mind, a form of hunting. I spent hours learning about the various designs of rifles, the purpose and use of telescopic sighting devices, and different kinds of ammunition. I learned that I could easily kill a large animal—or man—from several hundred yards away with the right gun allied with the right skill.

Considering that I expected to be operating in an urban environment, I puzzled over how I could deliver a deadly shot without being seen. I had already recognized that drive-by shooting, hiding in bushes, or lurking around the corner of a building all seemed impractical or even silly.

As I learned about the effective ranges of various rifles, I eventually arrived at the idea of firing from a stationary vehicle parked at least a half-block away from my target.

I quickly realized that I faced several decisions: not only what gun to buy but what ammunition and telescopic sight. I certainly needed a scope; having never fired a gun, I knew I needed any advantage to help me hit my target, fatally, with my first shot.

I also needed to figure out a way to practice shooting without my friends and colleagues knowing what I was doing. I didn't want anyone to know of my sudden uncharacteristic interest in long-range rifles. Finally, I needed a vehicle that could conceal me while I was executing my attack; the family Civic was not the right firing platform for my plans.

I reasoned that I needed the rifle to be short enough for easy handling inside a vehicle. My research led me to a Ruger American compact rifle. It was cheap, well-reviewed, and lightweight. With an available 18-inch barrel, it was also short enough for easy handling. Reviews claimed it had less recoil than models using heavier ammunition, which, for a novice like me, was reputed to translate into greater accuracy. Despite its lightness and the relatively small-caliber bullet, reviewer comments guaranteed its deadliness on sizable game like deer and hogs at least up to two hundred yards.

The one I bought came with a factory-installed scope. Further research led me to 95-grain bullets that expanded on contact, creating immense stopping power and "multiple wound channels." I liked the sound of that.

I ordered the rifle and a hundred rounds of ammunition online, then picked up the items at an outdoor-supply store in a town fifteen miles away to reduce the likelihood of running into a neighbor or acquaintance. I wasn't happy about having to provide personal information for the background check, but there was no alternative.

At home, I carefully studied the instructions for loading and handling the gun, practicing the bolt action until I was comfortable with it.

I had never been attracted to guns, but now that I had a need for one, I liked its heft, its black, no-nonsense matte finish, and its menacing aura of lethality. This device had but one purpose: to kill quickly and efficiently at a distance. Holding it, I felt a sense of power and agency I had never known.

Now I needed to learn how to use it. I located a shooting range twenty minutes from our house and went while Lauren was at work. I told the man running the range—a friendly, white-haired retiree named Bob—that I was new to shooting, and since there was nobody else there on a gray weekday morning, he helped me load the gun and sight the scope. I told him I was interested in deer hunting, and he recommended I sight the scope for two hundred yards.

Resting the gun on the cradle the range provided and following Bob's advice on breath control and how to smoothly squeeze the trigger, I found that at a hundred yards, most of my shots struck within inches of the bull's eye and sometimes even hit it. The scope and the stable gun cradle made accurate shooting far easier than I had anticipated. The recoil and noise, while startling at first, were easy to adjust to.

The key to accuracy, especially for a novice, Bob explained, was having a stable base to rest the gun on, so I decided to buy a tripod, which I brought to the range the next day. With Bob's help, I adjusted the tripod height to the right level for me, and with a little practice, I found myself placing shots in tight clusters at ranges between one and two hundred yards. Going to the range three times a week cemented my comfort with handling the gun and the tripod. As I progressed, Bob urged me to try shooting without resting the gun on a cradle or tripod, and while that was much harder, I began to master the skill after a few more visits.

Apparently impressed by my progress, Bob claimed I was a "natural" shooter, but I attributed my success to his guidance, the quality of the gun and the scope, and my intense motivation to learn. Whatever the reason, I now felt confident about being able to hit a static man-size target from at least two hundred yards.

But how was I to get within range of my target, carry out my mission, and get away without being identified? Considering the act I was contemplating, this was not a rhetorical question but a matter of life or death.

CHAPTER 6

I HAD TO ADMIT THAT I STILL WASN'T SURE I would be able to make myself carry out the deed I was practicing for, but I liked the way the sense of mission made me feel. It gave an urgency and purpose to my life that I had never experienced. Most of my life, I had drifted into whatever the next phase was: finish high school, go to college, then on to graduate school, because I was comfortable in academic settings. Marry a classmate, take the first job offer, and settle into an unremarkable domestic life in a quiet little college town. My parents had both died young from cancer, and Lauren's widowed father, a curmudgeon, lived in Seattle. We had learned to float along in our own warm little bubble that carried us easily over the few obstacles our comfortable middle-class American life presented.

Chris's drug crisis and death had exploded our bubble, and I could not envision myself settling quietly back into the rhythms of my former life. I was outraged by what had happened to us, and I embraced this outrage. At some level, I knew I was wrong to surrender to anger; I was willing to admit that I had been put to the test and had failed to respond in a proper, philosophical way. This was shameful, I suppose, because a man as well-educated as I was should be able to tap into wells of literature and philosophy to quench his anger. But I was unwilling. I relished the urge for revenge.

Notwithstanding my new focus on avenging my son, I had to live and maintain the appearance of normality. I was still teaching two classes at the college, but I was operating on autopilot. I knew my lack of commitment was unfair to my students, but I seemed incapable of mustering the energy and focus they deserved. I had also arrived at the awful realization that I resented the fact that my students—these vibrant, vivacious young people—were alive, but my son was not. Watching them laugh, joke, flirt, and even just walk and talk filled me with a deep, dull anger. A sense of unfairness washed over my capacity to manage what I knew was an irrational reaction.

The result was a class marred by a dull tension and occasional uncharacteristic sarcasm that I always regretted but couldn't seem to control. Students began avoiding me, attendance dropped, and the semester ended with fewer than half the students finishing my classes. I had always been a popular, successful teacher, and I felt sorry for what was clearly a failure, but the work I had always loved now seemed a distraction from my new purpose in life.

Fortunately, I had tenure, a well-established reputation, and, of course, the sympathy of the administration and my colleagues. They could see I was struggling, so at the end of the spring semester, the dean proposed a sabbatical on three-quarters pay for six months. This was a generous offer, and I readily accepted. The dean gently urged me to take a lengthy trip with Lauren to get my emotions stabilized and return to the college refreshed and energized.

Lauren, too, was struggling with her ability to focus on her part-time job as a medical billing consultant. She had always been a devoted and attentive mother and had taken the lead in the battle against Chris's addiction. Her sense of failure at his loss seemed even more profound than mine.

We had deeply enjoyed our roles as parents, but as Chris grew into his teenage years, Lauren, always a creative and restless spirit, had drifted away from me, focusing more on her art and environmental causes. The shift had been slow and subtle, but it eventually opened a widening gulf between us. My inclination toward solitary activities didn't help. We still loved each other—at least I loved her, I thought—but the ennui that seeps into so many marriages seemed to slowly but inexorably weaken our connection to one another.

Of course, we both had reveled in Chris's successes as a student and athlete, and then we became staunch, mutually supportive allies in his struggle with addiction. But his death, which was easy to view as our failure, had left us both feeling isolated. Other couples with stronger bonds may have reacted differently—I hope such couples exist—but our relationship had been weakened, not strengthened, by our tragedy.

I didn't recognize or understand this new reality at the time; grief and anger dominated my mind, leaving no room for subtler considerations. But I can look back now and see that I failed Lauren too. My consuming desire for revenge rendered me oblivious to her loneliness and need for care and attention.

And, of course, my absences, both physical and emotional,

exacerbated her loneliness. I had discovered a driving purpose, a mission, but Lauren had not. The loss of her son had plunged her into a deep, emotional abyss that I suppose only a mother could understand. But I should have tried to understand and taken steps to help her.

When Lauren found out I had been granted a generous sabbatical, she suggested that we start making plans for a lengthy trip somewhere overseas. This idea, while completely reasonable, obviously didn't align with my objectives, so I displayed false enthusiasm but took no action.

After a few days, Lauren realized I had not begun to research and formulate travel plans, as I had always done in the past, and began to question me in a gentle but persistent way. I knew I couldn't evade the subject for long and became so frustrated that her desires were at cross-purposes with mine that I was afraid I would lash out in anger if she asked again.

But then, perverse serendipity: Lauren's father had a stroke. Lauren's sister, her only sibling, had three young children and lived in a Chicago suburb, so her father's caregiver called to ask if Lauren could come to Seattle to help care for Ted.

To my relief, Lauren immediately decided to go. She urged me to go with her, but I resisted, claiming I didn't want to leave the house unoccupied for an indefinite period and asserting that some time alone might help me heal my grief and enable me to return to work sooner. After all, I pointed out, she hadn't been working much, and my three-quarters pay, while generous, was still likely to bury us in a deeper financial hole. We still owed huge debts for Chris's rehab care.

Lauren left the next day. I had mixed feelings about her indefinite absence and was decently concerned about Ted, hoping for his speedy recovery. My dominant emotion, however, was relief that a lengthy trip was off the table, and I could focus on my mission without interference or interruption. While I see my failure as a husband now, at the time my focus was on the only motivation that gave me the strength to get out of bed—vengeance.

My next step, I decided, was to acquire a vehicle that would serve as a shooting platform. I had been pondering the problem of a covert shooting site and had concluded that a van might be the answer. The right van would provide room in the back to establish a stable shooting position and would shield me from public view. With proper customization, it might even help dampen the noise of my gun's discharge. In addition, door-to-door delivery vans were ubiquitous in every neighborhood in every city and town, a fact that led me to hope that one more might pass unnoticed.

Finding a used van took me about a week. From a plumber, I bought a 2012 Chevrolet Express Cargo 1500, borrowing against money left from Chris's life insurance. It was white, with a six-cylinder engine, 61,000 miles, and good reliability ratings. The plumber had stripped off his company decals, and I liked its plainness; it was nondescript, like many other delivery vans. The seats were worn, but the tires were good. There were two dark windows in the back, and it had 225 cubic feet of cargo area, 52 inches high. Plenty of room to maneuver.

For a hundred dollars, plus another thirty or so for hardware, I found an off-duty car-window replacement mechanic who contrived a way to put the left rear window of the van on a hinge to raise and clip it open or shut as needed. I had told him I might need to carry long boards and other lengthy objects, a problem he solved easily for me.

Next, I bought foam-rubber anechoic panels online and glued them to the interior and ceiling of the cargo area. I had researched silencers for my rifle, but learned they would not actually silence the discharge, only muffle it somewhat. They were also expensive and required a registration process I didn't want to undertake. My hope was that firing from inside a van equipped with sound-suppressing foam would have a significant noise-dampening effect. Essentially, my idea was to turn the van itself into a silencer.

I needed to test my idea, so I drove the van into the woods on a colleague's property when I knew he and his wife were at work. Parked on a dirt road about a quarter mile from their house, I set up a series of tests using a decibel meter I bought online. For the first test, I placed the meter about forty yards down the road, directly behind the van. After opening the window, I set up my rifle on my tripod, with the muzzle tip about a foot inside the window, and fired a round. The meter measured the shot noise at only 90 decibels, much lower than the 140 I had expected based on my research. While still plainly audible, the shot was about as loud as a shout and quieter than the expensive suppressors I had researched would make it.

As I expected, the farther away I moved the meter, the quieter the shots became, and test levels to the sides and front of the van were very low, hardly likely to be noticed against a background of normal street noise. I also found that moving the gun deeper into the van reduced the noise even more. I was very happy with these results.

CHAPTER 7

AS SOMEONE WHO HADN'T HAD MUCH EXPERIENCE with practical problem solving, I felt a little proud of myself. On the way home, I bought a box of twenty rounds of ammunition. I was ready to visit the drug dealers I had met three months ago.

To save money, I slept in the van overnight on my way back to the city where Chris died and checked into an old motel on the fringe of my target neighborhood. Decent lodging close to campus was extremely expensive, and even this 1960s-era motel was overpriced, considering its utter absence of amenities. The only advantages it offered were proximity to my targets and the ability to park my van right in front of the door to my dim little room.

After checking into the motel around three, I decided to cruise the neighborhood. My goals were to see if the dealers I had identified were still doing business and to find other possible targets. I wanted to take out as many as I could as quickly as I could. It was a beautiful spring day, so I thought chances were good that they would be out in force.

I was gratified to see the stocky pusher I had first met calmly picking his teeth on his folding chair just where I left him. Two blocks over, I didn't see the Black pusher who had been glad to "help me out," but there was another young Black man in his place on a bench in front of a small market. I pulled over a block away. Within five minutes, I witnessed a transaction take place with a car full of what looked like teenagers.

As I drove the now-familiar streets, I spotted two new candidates and approached them with the confidence experience gave me. The first one, a heavily tattooed, slender young man with dark, glossy hair, eyed me suspiciously. I was wearing a T-shirt, ball cap, a three-day beard, and sunglasses, but still, no doubt, looked out of place.

To put him at ease and give him the impression I was a delivery driver, I rolled down the window and asked, "Hey, buddy, can you tell me where 221 Baker Street is?"

The young man, who had come to the passenger window, looked thoughtful, then said, "How about in London, smart ass?" I couldn't help but laugh.

"All right, you got me. What I really want to know is whether you might have something to sell."

"I might, but not to you."

"Come on, not even to a fellow *Sherlock Holmes* fan?"

"No way. You better move on."

"Okay, okay."

Outsmarted, I put the van in gear and drove deeper into the neighborhood. I soon spotted a tubby young man with dyed blond hair and an expensive-looking NBA warm-up suit jittering around on the sidewalk in front of a battered two-story frame house. As I got closer, I noticed his earbuds. He was swaying to music. When I pulled to the curb, he removed the earbuds and approached the van.

"Yo, what's up, my man?"

"I'm looking for some pain relief."

"Well, you came to the right place, boss. How much pain you need to get rid of?"

"Just a little, but I want the best stuff you got."

"Tell you what, swing around the block and slide back by here, and for twenty bucks, I'll give you what you need, boss man."

I did as instructed, and when I came back he extended his hand through the open window with a baggie dangling from his fingers. We made the exchange.

"Nice doing business with you, boss man."

As he turned away, I blurted out a question I thought he might answer, given how relaxed he seemed to be.

"I never saw so many dealers in one area. What's the story?"

"Oh, man, this ain't nothing compared to some of the places like Baltimore and KC, places like that. But here we got the college, the community college, warehouse workers, retired folks, all kinds of people who want to have a good time. You oughtta see this place on Friday night, when people are really ready to party!"

"So, when can I find you out here?" I asked.

"After three, count on it."

"Okay," I said.

My scouting had enabled me to identify one old target and three new ones. I decided, for now, to give the *Sherlock Holmes* fan a pass since I hadn't seen him moving any drugs, but I was sure of the other two. Tomorrow, I would "screw my courage to the sticking place" and do my best to execute them.

Pulling around to the back of the motel by an aromatic dumpster, I used two colors of electrical tape to alter my license number, turning an eight into a nine and a one into a seven.

Then, in the motel's tiny bathroom, I colored my hair black with a cheap, temporary dye. I had also procured a brown shirt and pants that, to a casual observer, might make me resemble an actual delivery man. I even had some sealed boxes in the van to further the ruse.

As events later showed, these efforts at disguise were unnecessary, maybe even nonsensical, but they made me feel more confident and better prepared, like an actor stepping into a new role.

As I did every night, I called Lauren for a perfunctory conversation that typically focused on her father's failing health. After a restless night, I awoke early, took a long walk, and breakfasted on scrambled eggs, toast, and grits at a surprisingly good diner filled with locals on their way to work.

CHAPTER 8

THE MORNING WAS OVERCAST BUT STILL WARM. I cruised the neighborhood but spotted no possible targets, so I spent the rest of the morning in the campus library. Then, after a fast-food lunch, I parked on the block where I had first bought the heroin-fentanyl mix from the gold-toothed dealer. I positioned the van about 120 yards away from where he normally sat, with a clear view of his duplex out the back windows. I opened the hinged back window, so as to not attract attention doing it later, and waited.

I was anxious, but strangely calm at the same time. I had thought through this scenario a thousand times, picturing the process in my mind's eye, so I felt well-prepared and confident. I did, however, remind myself that things rarely go exactly as planned.

About 1:30, I noticed that young men in ones and twos started showing up at the dealer's door, briefly stepping inside, then moving off purposefully. Some were on foot, others on bicycles and mopeds, two in a late-model SUV. At around 2:15, a bedraggled clump of four men and one middle-aged woman started loitering in front of the duplex. After a few minutes, I saw the dealer open his door and gesture to the waiting group. Money and envelopes changed hands, but he turned away one of the men, who then pursued another man, seeming to beg for a share of his drugs. Two of the men walked away with the woman.

The folding chair was in its usual place under the tree by the curb, but I had begun to worry that the pusher had changed his business practices and now operated only from his home. I was contemplating moving on to one of my other targets when, to my relief, he emerged from the duplex, crossed the dusty, littered yard, and, with what seemed like an air of resignation typical of a bored office worker, flopped onto the chair.

I had set up my tripod about three feet inside the van's cargo compartment and sat on a short, three-legged stool I had brought. I rested my rifle on the tripod and aimed through the open window. The muzzle was about two feet inside the van. My hands were shaking slightly, and I was perspiring more than usual, but resting the gun on the tripod and exercising breath control, I had my target in the crosshairs within fifteen seconds or so. He had his right leg across his left knee and his arms across his stomach as he chewed a toothpick.

I squeezed the trigger. Nothing happened. The safety was on! I was lucky because, as I turned it off and settled myself to take the shot, a low-slung black sedan pulled up to the curb in front of the dealer. I exhaled and realized instantly how stupid and fortunate I was. If I had pulled the trigger a few seconds earlier, the two men in the car would have been very likely to figure out the shot came from my van. As I breathed deeply to calm my rapidly beating heart, I warned myself to scan the area before trying again.

After about three minutes, the sedan pulled away, leaving the dealer stuffing something into his pocket. I carefully scanned the area and quickly eased back behind the gun. My target had resumed the same relaxed posture as before.

The bullet struck him in the upper middle of his chest. His arms flew out to the side, and the chair fell backward. He lay with one leg on the upended chair seat, arms splayed, unmoving.

I blinked, gathered myself, put the gun and tripod in the tool cabinet in the back of the van, lowered the window into place, and, clambering into the driver's seat, drove away slowly.

I was shaking a bit and filled with mixed feelings I was trying to sort out. One thing I was sure of was that I wasn't in shape to carry out another execution right away. I didn't want to go back to my depressing motel, so I decided to drive to a park on the other side of the campus to decompress. As I pulled into one of the many open parking spots and shut off the motor, I found myself overwhelmed by the urge to cry. I crawled into the cargo area and sobbed like a baby for what seemed like a long time. Then I fell into a deep sleep. When I awoke, the sun was setting with a soft amber glow, and the evening felt warmer than the day had been.

As I settled myself back in the driver's seat, I saw that the park was now crowded. Young men and women—college kids, I assumed—were everywhere. Couples were walking and talking; small groups lounged in circles on the grass, often laughing. It was a nice scene to wake up to.

But it clarified my thoughts and strengthened my resolve. These young people needed to be protected from the drug dealers, some of whom might be skulking around this very park. I got out of the van and walked the park's perimeter. To my surprise, I spotted no one who looked suspicious. I knew, however, where there were drug dealers, and my intention to exterminate them returned forcefully.

I was suddenly very hungry and decided to treat myself to a good meal. After changing at the motel, I found a well-regarded restaurant known for its prime rib, which I enjoyed with an excellent red wine.

Back at the motel, I had my brief evening conversation with Lauren, then turned on the local news and heard a cursory mention of the murder by gunshot of a man on West Durmont Street. That was my victim. They mentioned his name, but I immediately forgot it.

CHAPTER 9

I SPENT ANOTHER RESTLESS NIGHT troubled by strange dreams. Having breakfast at the diner, I inquired about getting a local newspaper. I learned that except for Wednesdays and Sundays, the "paper" was available only online. *Another stroke in the death of America*, I thought. I viewed the disappearance of local newspapers and the proliferation of hard drugs and pushers as markers of a decaying culture. I spent the rest of the morning and early afternoon at the campus library reading Dostoevsky. Then at 2 o'clock, I went into hunting mode.

My target this time was the talkative bleach-blond blowhard in the gaudy basketball jumpsuit. Like my first victim, he operated on a quiet neighborhood street, where, I calculated, with good timing and a little luck, I could put him out of business today.

By 2:30, I was parked on his street about 100 yards from where we had conducted our drug transaction. I felt calm, confident, and well prepared. The pusher made his appearance at 3:01, this time in a different NBA outfit enhanced by a big gold chain. He was on his cell phone, talking and gesturing. For the next forty-five minutes, he conducted business with buyers in cars and the occasional walk-up customer. I couldn't see much of the drive-up clientele, but the ones who arrived on foot looked, I thought, shabby and defeated. Maybe I was projecting my preconceived notions on them, but they conjured a mix of contempt and pity in me.

I was amazed by the pusher's brazen behavior as he reached into deep pockets and pulled out baggies of powder. He clearly wasn't afraid of observation or interference by the police. During the occasional lull in customer traffic, he would saunter into the faded house behind him to, I assumed, replenish his supplies.

Gradually, around 4 o'clock, the stream of buyers stopped. The pusher went into the house and emerged with a Mountain Dew, which he sipped on the concrete stoop of the house. This looked like my chance.

Surveying the area from the cab of the van, I could see no pedestrians or street traffic, so I quickly assumed my position behind my gun, fixed the dealer in my crosshairs, and squeezed the trigger. The bullet struck him just below the right armpit as he raised the drink to his mouth. He lurched sideways, and the bottle flew halfway across the dusty yard. He didn't move again.

As before, I stowed the tripod and gun in the cabinet, then slid into the driver's seat and eased the van slowly down the street. In a minute or so, I was on a busy avenue, safely away. Once again, I had no reason to think I had been observed. Buoyed by another success, I decided to try for a third the next day.

Over the following three days, I took out two more dealers in the same neighborhood a few blocks away from my first targets.

One I had killed instantly, I was sure. The other, a grossly rotund man I hit in the stomach, was on the ground but still moving his legs spasmodically as I drove away. I was fairly confident he would die, but even if he didn't, I had certainly put him out of business indefinitely.

Untroubled now by the waves of mixed emotions I had experienced after taking out my first target, I felt strong and—I had to admit—successful. I had identified a goal, made an action plan, and executed it to good effect. This was a new experience for me. I thought there was a high probability that one of the men I had shot had killed Chris but had to admit that I would never know for sure. Nevertheless, I felt that the steps I had taken were an appropriate response to the loss of my son.

The next day, like the previous three, brought perfect spring weather—sunny, warm, with a light breeze. But cruising through the neighborhood, I didn't see dealers anywhere. I felt I had become adept at identifying them—it wasn't hard—but now I couldn't spot any. Then I realized their disappearance made sense: fear of being shot had driven them all off the streets. Word had clearly gotten around that selling drugs had suddenly become very dangerous. To some extent, then, I had achieved more than revenge; I had single-handedly shut down the open-air drug bazaar in this notorious neighborhood.

I knew this cessation was bound to be temporary, but I felt good about it. These brazen death-dealers had been put on notice: there were consequences for their actions.

Well, I thought, *maybe it's time to go home.* I felt purged, lighter of spirit than I had since Chris's death. Maybe I could go back to being a sane man or what had previously passed for one.

My thoughts had recently turned more frequently to Lauren. I dutifully called her every evening, more out of obligation than a desire to talk. The calls were always the same, involving dismal details about her father's apparently hopeless medical state and cursory lies I fabricated about my activities around our house or the local gym. We had settled into a pattern of short conversations, since she had little to report other than her talks with medical personnel or old acquaintances I didn't know. I, of course, tried to keep my comments vague; the constant lying taxed my energy and creative powers. Nonetheless, our conversations felt like my only connection to a rational world, a world in which people acted on a decent concern for one another, the world I inhabited before drugs poisoned it.

Now that I had consummated my urge for revenge, I could feel the intensity of my anger waning, and Lauren's voice had begun to touch a deep part of me that I thought had withered to nothing. I realized I missed her and suddenly yearned to see her. A dawning desire to reconnect with her became my guiding purpose. I decided I would return to our home and get organized to go to Seattle to be with her.

CHAPTER 10

SATISFIED THAT I WAS DONE WITH MY REVENGE CAMPAIGN, I headed back to the motel, parked, and put the key in the door. Just as I did, a deep, forceful voice behind me said, "Police! Hold it right there!" Startled, I jerked, and my knees buckled, but I steadied myself. "Hands over your head," the man said. "Are you armed?"

I answered, "No." He quickly passed his hands over my torso and legs, extracting my wallet from my back pocket and my cell phone from my jacket as he finished.

"All right, in!" he ordered.

Shaking, I opened the door. If I hadn't already inserted the key, I don't think I could have done it. I was trembling too intensely with shock and fear. The room was unlit, the blinds closed, as I had left them, but I could discern a heavyset man sitting in the one chair the room provided.

He said, "Sit on the bed. We need to talk." I did, grateful to be off my quivering legs. The first man, who had followed me in, handed him my wallet and phone.

"No weapons," he told the seated man, who nodded.

The seated man looked to be about fifty years old. He wore a dark gray suit that appeared uncomfortably tight across his thick shoulders. His neck, constrained by a maroon tie and white shirt, bulged above his collar. His reddish, jowly face was topped by short, thinning gray hair. The other man, by contrast, was lean and muscular in a black T-shirt, jeans, and a lightweight blue jacket. He was square-jawed and had high cheekbones, black shoulder-length hair, and alert, dark eyes trained tightly on me.

The seated man calmly pulled my license from my wallet and studied it. It looked tiny in his scarred, sausage-like fingers. Incongruously, his thick wrist bore a Rolex on a silver band.

"So, Mister William Vere Larson, you're the man we have to thank for the sudden decline in local drug sales." It was a statement, not a question. My mind raced as I tried to think of a way to plausibly deny it. In a quivering voice, I ended up offering a reply that sounded ridiculous even to me. "I don't know what you mean."

The big man gave a short chuckle. "Oh, I think you do, Mr. Larson. Can I call you Bill?"

Feeling like I was in a bad film noir movie, I told him, "I go by my middle name."

"Vere it is, then. Unusual name."

"My father was a Melville fan. Vere was the captain in *Billy Budd*."

"Okay, well—Vere—as it turns out, I'm a captain too. The police captain in charge of our fair city's special drug enforcement department." He pulled back his jacket to reveal a gold badge on his shirt.

He gestured to the younger man. "This gentleman is one of our finest plain-clothes agents. At this point, we don't think it would be helpful to tell you our names. I hope you understand."

I found his exaggerated courtesy strangely menacing. Slightly calmer now, I said, "I have to admit that I don't understand. Am I under arrest?"

"No, you aren't, Vere. But you certainly will be if you don't provide certain responses we're looking for."

"Okay," I said.

"Let's start with the fact that we know you're the guy who's taken out at least three, maybe four, of our local street dealers."

He paused and looked at me as if he expected me to confirm what he said, but I didn't. With a brief look of mild annoyance, he continued, "Let's get on the same page here, Vere. You might as well admit it because Officer Rodriguez—Damn! I didn't mean to say that. Anyway, he saw you take down Buggy Chamorro last Tuesday, then trailed you while you stalked another dealer the next day. He followed you here yesterday, so let's not play games. You're the guy."

"All right," I said, feeling a mixture of fear and relief after admitting the truth.

"Good! Now that we got that out of the way, I gotta ask, why? You're not a hit man from one of the gangs because you've been very, let's say, undiscriminating—you killed guys from two different gangs. You didn't rob them; you just shot 'em. So why? What's this about?"

"I believe a dealer around here sold drugs that killed my son."

The big man pursed his lips and said, "Hm! So your son died of an overdose." I nodded. "And this was your idea of payback..."

"Retribution, yes."

"Ah, yes, righteous retribution. Okay. Well, I hope you got some satisfaction out of it, Vere, because you could kill a hundred street dealers and it wouldn't make any difference. They're like roaches. You kill one, three others are ready to take their place. Most of 'em are ex-cons who can't do anything else. Or won't."

I shrugged. "I wanted to do something."

He nodded thoughtfully. "You really want to do something? Something that can make a real difference?"

"Yes," I said truthfully.

He looked at me for a few long seconds. "That's why we're talking to you instead of taking you downtown right now. You've done something a lot of us cops wish we could do—you took out some low-life pushers. A lot of us dream of doing that, but legally, of course, we can't. Fact is, there's not much point anyway. To really hurt 'em, you got to go after the bosses. To be exact, you have to go after one boss in particular to make a difference around here."

I thought I could see where this was going, but wasn't sure.

"You seem to know what you're doing. What are you, a retired Army sniper or something?"

I couldn't help laughing a little. "No, self-taught, more or less."

"Hm! Rodriguez says he thinks you're using some kind of silenced rifle. That right?"

"The van is the silencer. I just make sure I'm far enough inside that most of the sound gets captured by the cargo box itself. I have it lined with soundproofing panels."

"Interesting. Smart. How'd you learn to do that?"

"Just figured it out." He nodded, seeming mildly impressed. "You done anything like this in other cities?"

"No, this is it. My son was at the university."

"Too many kids are ODing these days. It's terrible."

I nodded, surprised that I was close to tearing up.

He leaned toward me and, in a soft voice, said, "Let's do something about it, Vere."

"That's what I came here for," I said with a catch in my voice that surprised me.

He exchanged a look with the impassive Rodriguez.

The big police captain said, "Look, you've already hurt the two local gangs in a way you might not have realized. They're going to war because they each think the other is poppin' their street dealers. The trouble is, when the gangs go to war, innocent people tend to get hurt, murder rates rise, the TV starts getting the citizens riled up, and city hall gets on our ass. So, while it's bad for the gangs, it's also bad for me and my officers and any folks who get caught in the crossfire, as some always do. So, since you've brewed up a shitstorm for us, Vere, I'm glad you're open to helping."

"So what would you like me to do?"

"Cut the head off the snake. His name's Vincente Chamorro. He's the boss of the biggest gang in the state."

"And you want me to take him out..."

"Exactly."

Puzzled, I asked, "Is he a street dealer? Doesn't sound like he would be."

"No, not hardly. He supplies the drugs to most of the dealers. Got dozens working for him. Take him out, we put a serious dent in the flow of drugs. You know that kid in the basketball outfit, blond hair? That was his nephew, Buggy. Our sources tell us Chamorro is ragin' around the streets, way more visible than usual. We might have a chance to pop him."

"How?"

"That's where you come in. See, we think he usually stays in Mexico, but he's come up here to go to his nephew's funeral, rally his troops, and, as we hear it, go to war with the Trujillo gang, who he blames for killing Buggy. We think you might get a chance at him at the funeral home. We take him out, we're hoping his whole operation falls apart: less drugs on the street and no war."

"Won't he be expecting an attempt to kill him? By the other gang, I mean. Won't he take precautions?"

"Sure he will, but we have a plan to put you in the right spot at the right time."

"Why can't you just arrest Chamorro?"

"That sounds good—in theory—but Chamorro is no amateur. He knows how to keep lots of layers between him and the street drugs. We know a lot about him from informants, but not enough that would stand up in court to get him convicted of anything."

I nodded.

"So, we think our best chance at him will be tomorrow afternoon outside the funeral home where the viewing will take place. We have a source who tells us Chamorro is planning to come in the back way, not the main door everybody else is using. There's a motel behind the funeral home, and we've got a room where the window will give you a good shot at the back door."

"So, no van?"

"No van. We want you to use your rifle, though."

"But here's the thing. I've only taken out guys who were pretty much standing still, with no idea they were in danger. And I had plenty of time to set up my shot. This is different. This man—Chamorro—knows he might be in danger and will probably be moving fast. I'm not at all confident I can pull this off."

The big man digested my comment, then said, "You're obviously a smart guy. You'll figure it out."

I just looked at him.

He went on, "Look, nothing's a guarantee. Just remember, you take care of this, and we'll make sure you stay a free man."

I asked, "What hope do I realistically have of getting away with this?"

"There's a high chain-link fence between the motel and the funeral home. Even if they figure out where the shot comes from, you should still have plenty of time to get out before any of them can get you. And Rodriguez will be there to help look after you."

I nodded, feeling like the room was a box I was trapped in.

The big man went on, "The viewing's at one tomorrow. You need to be in place by twelve, latest. Rodriguez will pick you up here at, what, eleven-fifteen?" he asked, looking at Rodriguez.

Rodriguez nodded.

The big man turned back to me. "Vere, I'm going to leave you here, trusting that you'll be ready to go tomorrow and that you'll do what we've talked about. You understand that if you don't, we'll find you, arrest you, convict you, and you'll go to prison for a long time, which, by the way, you won't finish, because once the local boys find out you killed their dealers, your days on earth are probably in the single digits."

"But if I succeed in taking out Chamorro?"

"You'll be free to go. As long as you keep your mouth shut, leave our fair city, and don't come back. The honest citizens around here don't give a shit about a few low-life dealers getting popped, but we don't need a self-appointed vigilante stirring up trouble. Do we understand each other?"

"Yes," I replied, wondering, as I had when Chris died, how life can change so quickly.

He handed back my wallet but passed my phone to Rodriguez, saying, "Note the number. For tracking if we need it." Rodriguez did, then returned my phone.

"Good hunting tomorrow, Vere," the big man said.

He towered over me as he stood up, well over six feet, and, I guessed, nearly three hundred pounds. He moved easily, though, as he walked to the door. As he passed Rodriguez, he said to him, "You know what to do. Call me when it's over."

Rodriguez nodded, watched the big man walk out, and closed the door.

"So, your son died of an overdose?"

I nodded.

"Fentanyl?"

"Yes."

"How old?"

"Just turned nineteen."

"Happens too much around here. He was at the college, right?"

"He died on his second day there." I was surprised and somehow gratified by his interest in my son.

"So, did you have any idea he was into drugs?"

"He'd just gotten out of a long stay in rehab. We thought he'd be okay as long as he stayed away from his local sources back home, but obviously we were wrong. And he had just lost his girlfriend, so we think maybe that's what pushed him back to the drugs, but who knows? The investigating detective told us he probably took a walk and ran into one of the street dealers."

"Who was the detective?"

"Moreland."

"He's okay. One of the better ones. But the truth is, your son could've bought that stuff right on campus. There's guys who go to school over there just to be close to the kids, especially to the girls. The college police usually figure it out after a while, but the school tries to keep it quiet if they can. Anyway, it's a big problem. I'm sorry about your boy. This damn fentanyl is everywhere now. If the dealers mix it wrong with the other drugs, well..."

"Yeah..."

After a pause, Rodriguez asked, "So you up for this thing tomorrow? Baxter made it sound easy, but believe me, it could get dodgy real fast. We gotta know what we're doing."

"Doesn't sound like I have much choice. But, to be honest, I'm not sure I can pull it off. Like I said, the guys I shot were all standing still, by themselves on a quiet street. Chamorro is going to be moving, and he's bound to have other people around him—bodyguards, maybe family members."

Rodriguez said, "Bodyguards, for sure. Family, maybe not. They might go in the main door, but you're right, we don't know."

I said, "By the way, shouldn't we disguise ourselves in some way? I mean, we don't want the people working at the motel to be able to ID us."

"I have a key that'll open any door in the place, so we can use the side entrances. And I've set up everything so far by phone, so they don't know what I look like. But, for sure, we don't want anybody IDing us."

"Do they have surveillance cameras?"

"It's not the kind of place that would have cameras, but if they do, I'll have them turn them off while we're there. The good news is that at one in the afternoon the place should pretty much be empty. The Downtown Inn isn't exactly a vacation destination."

I was somewhat reassured by Rodriguez's friendliness and eagerness to collaborate. Only later did I learn that Baxter had told him to win my trust. Of course, success in this assassination attempt was important to him too, so collaboration was sensible.

Rodriguez suggested, "Let's go over there so you can check the place out. Just so you know, the motel manager thinks we just want to surveil Chamorro and take pictures."

We rode in his late-model silver Camaro, provided by the city's taxpayers. At my suggestion, we stopped at a thrift store so I could buy a gray raincoat long enough to conceal my rifle.

CHAPTER 11

THE DOWNTOWN INN WAS A LONG, three-story building with a large, littered parking lot between a transmission repair shop and a self-storage business. Across the street was the Handy Pawnshop and Faith Deliverance Tabernacle, sandwiched between an empty laundromat and a four-story brick building that showed scorch marks above plywood-covered windows. These dilapidated relics of better times reminded me of solid citizens bruised and battered in a bar fight. I wondered, as I often had, whether the dealers sold drugs mainly in poor neighborhoods, or whether the neighborhoods became poor because the dealers sold drugs in them.

Rodriguez pulled into a spot close to the west end of the motel. Plastic liquor bottles and fast-food debris decorated the corners of the entrance alcove. I put on my ball cap and sunglasses and, once through the door, followed him left through a fire door and up the steps, observed, as far as I could tell, by no one. Neither of us noticed any hallway cameras.

Rodriguez recommended a firing position on the second floor, to aid in a speedy getaway. He had already been assured by the manager that all the rooms, except for one on the third floor, were empty.

Using his master key, we checked six rooms until we found the one with the most direct view of the funeral home's rear entrance. From this vantage point, the shot would be only forty yards, maybe less. Unlike the funeral home's front entrance, this doorway was not shielded by an awning, so our target would be in the clear until he went through the door.

We checked the windows, which, after a little persuasion, swung outward almost perpendicular to the wall. Gauging the angles, I felt confident I could fire from deep enough in the room that my rifle barrel wouldn't be visible from below. I was pleased to see an eight-foot chain-link fence around the perimeter of the funeral home's parking lot. I guessed the owners had erected it to protect their patrons' cars from break-ins, but now it promised to help protect me, at least briefly, from men of murderous intent. My firing position was high enough that the fence wouldn't hinder my shot.

Our scouting trip done, we exited the same way we had entered, again encountering no one. Hungry, we ordered burgers from a fast-food takeout window and ate them in my motel room. I was surprised that Rodriguez joined me to eat, but he seemed to want the company. Or maybe he was still trying to assess my resolve and reliability. A couple of times, I noticed him studying me, but then he would glance away.

After quickly finishing his meal, he announced, "I'm out. I'll be here by eleven tomorrow."

"Okay." I nodded.

After he left, I sat for at least twenty minutes, pondering my situation. Cliché, of course, but events had developed so quickly and strangely that I honestly felt like I would be waking up from a dream any moment. But the reality was that I was in extreme peril—the most dangerous situation of my life. If I tried to flee, I doubted I would make it out of the city; for all I knew, Baxter or Rodriguez had me under observation right now, and they had my cell phone number, which I guessed they could use to track my location—unless I destroyed it. I didn't know much about cell phone tracking, but I supposed that even destroying my phone might alert them that I planned to flee. And, of course, they could have easily attached a tracking device to my van. So, running did not seem like a viable option. They had me between the sword and the wall.

As far as I could see, my only hope was to succeed in assassinating Chamorro and hope that Baxter would keep his promise to let me go. I had genuine concerns about being able to accomplish the assassination, but I resolved to do my best to pull it off. After all, my elimination of a few street thugs was, as Baxter had pointed out, insignificant in the scheme of things, whereas liquidating a drug lord might actually make a difference. Again, though, while killing Chamorro might be a temporary setback for the local drug trade—and might help satisfy what had begun to feel like an inane urge for pointless revenge—in truth, it was more like cutting one head off a hydra; the others would continue to thrive. But I was committed. I saw no way out.

I called Lauren with an underlying sense of urgency, not knowing if this might be the last time I talked with her. After getting the usual depressing report on her dad, I found myself telling her how much I missed her and declaring that I wanted to join her soon.

She replied, "I would like that. Hey, are you okay? You sound stressed. Everything okay there?"

"I'm fine. Just realizing how much I miss you."

"Well, I miss you too. When do you think you could head out?"

"Week or so, maybe. I have a few things to take care of first."

"What kind of things?"

"Just odds and ends." *Especially "ends," I thought. Chamorro's and maybe mine.* "I could tell you about them when I see you."

"Well, I don't understand the vagueness, but okay. As long as you're sure everything's all right."

"Yes, all's okay."

"Hey, Dad's monitor is beeping. I better go."

"All right. Hey . . . I love you."

After a pause, "I love you too, Vere."

Even though we were separated by about two thousand miles, I felt closer now to Lauren than I had for months. *Maybe*, I thought, *the hard spot in me has melted enough to let more positive impulses flow again.*

CHAPTER 12

I SLEPT VERY LITTLE THAT NIGHT. Various scenarios played out in my mind: *What if I miss Chamorro? What if I hit one of his bodyguards, or, worse yet, a member of his family or a funeral home employee? What if we don't get out of the motel and into the car in time? What if I stumble rushing down the stairs and break my ankle? Will Rodriguez abandon me?* These and more fantastic possibilities raced through my mind, urgent but unanswerable. I finally fell asleep just before dawn and awoke a couple of hours later, wired and vibrating.

In the van, I fully loaded the magazine of the Ruger and left it and my tripod where I could quickly access them. I paid the motel bill and then, after buying coffee and an egg sandwich at the diner, ate and waited in my motel room.

Rodriguez arrived early, about 10:45. With a strange, pinched look on his face, he said he had to talk to me.

"We're gonna have to move fast after we do our thing today, so

I figured I better talk to you now." He took a deep breath, looked at the floor, then gazed directly into my eyes and said, "I'm supposed to kill you after you shoot Chamorro."

He had my attention.

"But I'm not going to," he continued.

I felt like thanking him but resisted.

"Here's the situation: Baxter and I have been working together for the past three years or so, ever since I joined the antidrug division, so called. Not long after I joined, Baxter and a couple other longtime guys sat me down at his house and explained how the system works. Bottom line, everybody makes money on the drug trade. You arrest a dealer, you keep most of the cash you confiscate, and make sure Baxter gets his cut. Some of the money comes from payoffs for *not* arresting guys. Plus, some cops keep drugs they confiscate, supposedly to pay off informants, who tend to be junkies, but some—a few—actually sell the drugs to addicts and maybe even other dealers. I don't know for sure, 'cause I never do that. I know some other guys do, though. Anyway, Baxter made it clear how the game was played and what, let's say, the penalties would be if I wasn't in the game with 'em. So, I've been on the receiving end of a pretty steady stream of cash for the past few years."

I asked, "So, is everybody crooked?"

"No. I'm not sure how they make it work, but some cops don't seem to be at the table. They keep quiet, though, about the guys who are. Too unhealthy not to."

"Why does Baxter want me dead? Because I took out a few low-level dealers?"

"The main thing he wants is for you to eliminate Chamorro. I've thought for a while that he was working for Trujillo because we almost never hit his operation. Now I'm sure of it. With Chamorro out of the picture, Trujillo is the top dog. If Baxter can make that happen, who knows what goodies Trujillo will send his way. You came along, and Baxter, who's a smart guy, figured out right away that he could use you. You've proven you can do the job, and you're a stranger with no connection to anybody. Clean and simple. A godsend for Baxter. Trouble is, you would be able to connect him to Chamorro's murder, and Baxter doesn't like loose ends. You would be a loose end, so you need to be cut off."

After I spent a few seconds processing his explanation, I asked the obvious question. "So, how come you're not going to kill me?"

"I'm not a killer. Baxter thinks I am because I took down two thugs on a drug raid once. But they were trying to kill me. This is different. It's one thing to skim a little cash out of the system, but he can't make me do cold-blooded murder. Besides, I got into policing because I honestly wanted to make a difference. My older sister and my favorite cousin OD'd and died, so I get what you've been doing and how you feel about your son. I might be bent a little, but I'm not crooked like Baxter. And I think I might have a chance to use this situation to get rid of him."

"How?"

"By using my informants to tell Chamorro's people that Baxter was behind this hit. Then I'll just let nature take its course."

"You think getting rid of Baxter could make things better?"

"Maybe. They can't get much worse. And if something happens to him, other crooked cops might not show so much love to the gangs. The way I see it, Baxter's gotta go, or I gotta go. I can't have him making me his tool. God only knows what he'll want me to do if he thinks I'll kill anybody he wants me to. The trick is, we gotta make Baxter think I killed you. It's the only way me and you survive."

"I see. So how can we make that work?"

"I've thought a lot about it, and here's what I came up with. We do the hit on Chamorro, you disappear, back to wherever you came from, which, by the way, I don't wanna know. I tell Baxter I killed you and dumped you and your van in a lake outside the city. You're gone and hopefully safe, and I talk to my informants."

"Is there any way I can help? Other than disappearing, which I will be glad to do."

"No. Oh, yeah, you'll have to lose your cell phone. Tonight sometime, so it's like it went into a lake."

"That makes sense. Small sacrifice for me."

"Okay, that's the plan. We do Chamorro, you disappear, I tell Baxter you're dead, then we hope Chamorro's guys will take care of Baxter after my informants rat him out."

"Rodriguez," I said.

"Yeah?"

"Thank you."

"Well, we do this right, it'll help both of us. And maybe a lot of other people too. Okay?"

"Okay."

"All right, I brought some photos of Chamorro."

On the threadbare carpet, he spread out three eight-by-ten color photos of a chunky, middle-aged man with thinning black hair and a thick black mustache. Chamorro was dressed in a cream-colored suit over an open-collar white shirt. He was exiting a private plane.

"Ready to do this?" Rodriguez asked.

"Ready as I'll ever be, I guess."

I'm sure I sounded more resigned than confident because Rodriguez said, "Look, this is scary shit, but you can do it—and it's for a good cause, especially considering what happened to your kid. Just think about that."

I nodded, looking around the motel room to make sure I hadn't left anything—I had already put my travel bag in the van—and we exited. Rodriguez had parked close to my van, so I quickly transferred my rifle and tripod into the Camaro.

At the Downtown Inn, Rodriguez backed into the spot closest to the south entrance. We put on hats, surgical gloves, and sunglasses and made our way to the room we had selected the day before. While I set up my shooting position, Rodriguez went to open windows in some other rooms on our floor and the floor above. I had suggested this ploy in the hope of confusing Chamorro's men about the source of our shots.

We had about an hour before the viewing. I adjusted and readjusted my tripod, checked my rifle repeatedly, and finally had to tell myself to calm down. I used a breathing exercise to steady myself and surrendered to the situation. I was in it. There was nothing sensible I could do about it, so I resigned myself to it. Whatever happened could not be as awful as losing my son. I thought of calling Lauren but realized she would probably detect the strain in my voice, and I didn't want to spend energy on evasions or explanations. I needed to stay focused.

Rodriguez rejoined me, and we watched as cars began to fill the funeral home's side parking lot, which we could see from our vantage point. Most of the mourners were dressed conservatively, but a few wore low-slung jeans and open shirts, augmented by heavy gold chains and ballcaps. A priest arrived, greeted obsequiously by two dark-suited men I had identified as funeral-home employees.

Rodriguez provided a running commentary on the attendees.

"There's Frankie Guiterrez, a two-bit street dealer I've personally busted twice. And wait a minute—that's Dr. Galvez! He runs a pharmacy near West Lake. Whoa! I'm going to have to look into his connection with the Chamorros. That's definitely a surprise!" Rodriguez recognized at least five of Chamorro's gang, as well as some of the more ostensibly respectable citizens.

While I found his commentary interesting, I was concerned that there were numerous children in attendance. I had already decided that I wouldn't take a shot if children or women might get hit. I didn't even like the idea of exposing innocent people, especially children, to a traumatic event. Despite these misgivings, though, I was committed to killing Chamorro if I could.

The lot was almost full when the back door of the funeral home opened and a self-important-looking middle-aged man exited, talking animatedly on his cell phone. A moment later, two shiny black Range Rovers wheeled into the parking lot and, following the directions of arm-waving funeral home employees who held back pedestrian mourners, rolled up to the funeral home's back door.

Rodriguez, visibly excited, hoarsely whispered, "This is it! This has got to be Chamorro. Get ready!"

I slid off the safety, pressed the rifle butt firmly against my shoulder, and sighted just beyond the back left door of the first car, guessing that's where Chamorro could be. I had to assume that the funeral director would recognize Chamorro and planned to use him to quickly identify my target. I was counting on Rodriguez as a second pair of eyes too.

As the cars jerked to an abrupt stop, all the passenger doors sprang open and five men in dark suits emerged. Four immediately paused and scanned the area, while the fifth reached to open the door of the first vehicle, as I had anticipated. One of the bodyguards fixed his gaze momentarily on the motel windows, then looked to the roof, then back to the parking lot. At that moment, Chamorro exited the Range Rover. "That's him!" Rodriguez blurted.

Casually buttoning his suit jacket, Chamorro paused to shake hands with the head-bobbing funeral director. The pause, though only a second or two, gave me the opportunity I needed.

I was aiming for his upper back, but Chamorro's slight turn to shake hands and my lack of experience in shooting from a height caused me to hit him in his neck, right below his left ear. Blood sprayed the funeral director and the nearest bodyguard as Chamorro collapsed violently onto the pavement. A bodyguard fell too, possibly struck by the bullet passing through Chamorro.

As I turned away from the window, Rodriguez smacked me on the back, declaring, "You did it! Now let's get the hell outta here!"

I didn't need encouragement. I collapsed the tripod, slid it and the rifle under my long coat, and exited the room in seconds. We ran through the hall, down the steps, and were in Rodriguez's car in less than half a minute. We had parked out of sight of the funeral home, so I couldn't see what was happening as Rodriguez drove quickly but smoothly away. He went through a red light at the nearest corner, and we quickly blended into the light traffic.

"That was incredible! You definitely took out Chamorro!"

I didn't tell him that the shot had been a lucky one. I was shaking and decided I wanted to be done with shooting people, even ones who were evil. Two police cars, lights flashing and sirens blaring, raced past us toward the funeral home.

Back at my motel, Rodriguez dropped me beside my van.

"Remember to destroy your phone," he reminded me.

"I will."

He extended his hand, and I shook it.

"Good job," he said. "I wasn't sure you could pull it off."

"I wasn't either," I replied. "Thanks for being a decent cop. You've given me hope."

He replied, "And you've given *me* hope. Look after yourself." He sped quickly out of the parking lot and down the block.

I threw my rubber gloves and thrift-store coat into the motel dumpster, tore the tape off my license plate to restore the correct number, climbed in the van, and started the long drive home.

About an hour out of the city, I spotted a lake that was part of a state park and meandered down a winding two-lane road to a small empty parking lot. I scanned for cameras and, seeing none, made my way to the edge of a broad inlet with thickly forested shores. A few fishermen in boats were scattered on the lake, but since it was a weekday, no one else was around.

Walking the lake shore, I found what looked like a deep spot, so I went back to the van, retrieving my phone, rifle, tripod, and ammunition. I smashed my phone with the rifle, wiped everything down with paper towels, and threw them all as far out in the lake as I could. A curve in the shoreline concealed me from any fishermen.

Earlier, I had paused at a truck stop to email Lauren that I had "lost" my phone and that she wouldn't hear from me for a day or two, so I wasn't worried about being without a phone for now.

CHAPTER 13

I FELT A CURIOUS SENSE OF FREEDOM, a lightness that was fresh to me. Throwing the gun away lifted a weight I hadn't realized I was carrying. I felt no guilt about killing the men I had shot, but I had a growing awareness that murdering them had indelibly stained my soul. I wasn't a religious man and had no worries about divine retribution, but I had been what might be called a decent man, and now I no longer felt I was.

I wanted to be done with violence. The canker on my spirit had been lanced, the poison released. I had to pack this experience into a dark corner of my psyche and lock it there. Whether I could do that and resume a semblance of my former life remained to be seen.

I believed salvaging my relationship with my wife was the key to meeting this challenge. I decided I would muster the same focus, inventiveness, and determination to restore our former connection that I had brought to wreaking vengeance. Only this time, I would be motivated not by hate but by love.

After an uneventful drive home, I immediately acquired a new phone with a different number and was back in touch with Lauren. Now that my focus was truly on her, our conversations became deeper, richer, and more rewarding than they had been in years. I promised her I would soon join her in Seattle, and she, perhaps impressed by the honest attention I was giving her, seemed more receptive than she had been.

On the second night after my return home, I had another dream. Lauren and I were holding hands on the edge of the same frozen river that swallowed young Chris in my previous dream. This time, though, across the river at the edge of a dark, snow-filled forest, teenage Chris stood in his blue and gray high school baseball uniform, his blue cap in his right hand, his glove on his left. He looked at us, raised his cap in a kind of salute, and then put it firmly on his head as we had so often seen him do. He smiled, waved, looked at us a moment longer, then turned and disappeared into the woods. On the frozen river between us, a dead crow lay. I woke with a sense of peace.

Over the next few days, I sold the van to a local car dealer, settled bills, and arranged my flight to Seattle. I had subscribed online to the newspaper of the city where Chris had died and carefully reviewed the local events there daily. One short but chilling article reported the murder of the manager of the Downtown Inn. He had been shot several times at point-blank range. The police had no suspects.

A few days later, as I was reading the online paper in the concourse of our local airport, a headline leaped out at me: "Police Captain and Wife Die in Fiery Explosion." Baxter was gone. Apparently, Rodriguez's plan had worked. Unknown assassins had gotten into

Baxter's garage and wired his car with a bomb. Baxter had been right; in drug wars, innocent people die. In this case, his wife. The police chief and politicians were vowing swift apprehension of the culprits and possible assistance from federal authorities.

Over the next few months, as I followed the progress of the case, numerous low-level criminals were arrested, and the city's homicide rate shot up as a full-scale gang war broke out. My actions had led to ripple effects I had not foreseen. Then I read that Lieutenant Emmanuel Rodriguez had been elevated to the role that the late Captain Baxter had vacated: head of the city's antidrug division. In a press conference, he pledged to break the hold of the drug gangs and vigorously root out corruption.

Whether that happened, I don't know.

EPILOGUE

SHORTLY AFTER I JOINED LAUREN IN SEATTLE, her father died. I helped her and her sister plan the service and settle their father's affairs. Ted left Lauren and her sister almost half a million dollars each, as well as a large home Lauren and I might buy from her sister. I applied for a teaching position at the local colleges and have had two promising interviews.

Since my employment wasn't urgent or imminent, Lauren suggested we venture out on a short vacation. While driving to Alaska in the Escalade she inherited, I mentioned that I heard Alaska is a renowned state for hunting. Lauren replied, "Hunting! So what? You're no hunter!"

I smiled to myself and said, "You're right. Let's forget that."

The highway stretched in front of us, a narrow strip through vast, green forests thick with secrets and possibilities.

ACKNOWLEDGEMENTS

I'll be forever grateful to my daughter Melissa, my friends Ellen and Pamela, and my sweet wife Susan, for supporting me with intelligence, kindness, and encouragement.

www.ingramcontent.com/pod-product-compliance
Lightning Source LLC
LaVergne TN
LVHW041713060526
838201LV00043B/715